ROAD TRIP
FUN TIME

by Wrigley Stuart

illustrated by Patrick Spaziante

CARTOON NETWORK BOOKS

An Imprint of
Penguin Random House

CARTOON NETWORK BOOKS
Penguin Young Readers Group
An Imprint of Penguin Random House LLC

Photo credits: page 60: [recreational vehicle] moodboard/Thinkstock; page 61:
[convertible] olejnik/iStock/Thinkstock, [sports car] andrii lurlou/Hemera/Thinkstock,
[pickup truck] bsauter/iStock/Thinkstock, [jeep] jacoblund/Thinkstock;
page 96: [map] sky_max/iStock/Thinkstock; page 100: [tractor] Purestock/Thinkstock;
page 101: [motorcycle] Dunca Daniel/Hemera/Thinkstock, [school bus] mokee81/
iStock/Thinkstock, [cement truck] qingwa/iStock/Thinkstock,
[taxis] Uladone/iStock/Thinkstock.

ISBN 9780515159240

10 9 8 7 6 5 4 3 2 1

HEY, GUYS.
WELCOME TO THE RUST
BUCKET. IT'S OUR HOME AWAY FROM
HOME. ACTUALLY, IT SORT OF FEELS
MORE LIKE HOME THAN HOME. WE'RE
TRAVELING THE COUNTRY, AND IT SEEMS
LIKE EVERYWHERE WE GO, A HORRIBLE
VILLAIN IS PLOTTING WORLD
DESTRUCTION.

It never gets boring saving the world, but sometimes it can get a little dull traveling to places. I play a lot of video games since it can be hard finding fun things to do.

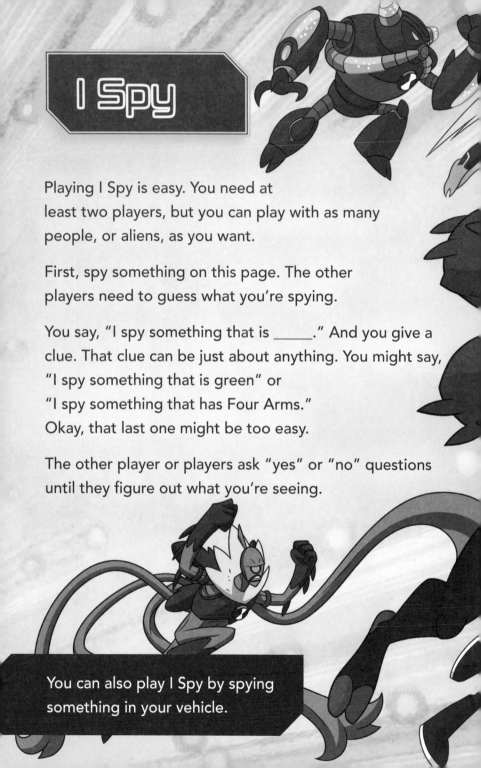

I Spy

Playing I Spy is easy. You need at least two players, but you can play with as many people, or aliens, as you want.

First, spy something on this page. The other players need to guess what you're spying.

You say, "I spy something that is _____." And you give a clue. That clue can be just about anything. You might say, "I spy something that is green" or "I spy something that has Four Arms." Okay, that last one might be too easy.

The other player or players ask "yes" or "no" questions until they figure out what you're seeing.

You can also play I Spy by spying something in your vehicle.

CAN YOU HELP BEN FIND ZOMBOZO?

Zombozo plans to destroy the entire city unless one of Ben's aliens can stop him! Unfortunately, Ben totally lost sight of him. Can you help Ben find Zombozo while avoiding his minions?

Twenty Questions

WITH MY INTELLECT, I USUALLY ONLY NEED THREE QUESTIONS TO GUESS THE ANSWER. BUT YOU'RE NOT AS SMART AS ME, SO YOU MIGHT NEED ALL TWENTY.

Think of something—anything in the world (or out of the world)—and the other players have to guess what it is. They can only ask "yes" or "no" questions and only have twenty questions to guess it. They can ask anything, like "Is it an animal?" or "Is it an alien with twenty eyeballs?"

- Guessers will want to be broad in their first questions and then try to narrow it down.

- You can establish rules before you begin, such as "it must be a real thing" or "it must be found in this car."

- Don't waste a question! The final guess counts as one of the twenty questions.

Road Trip Alphabet

A _____   K _____

B _____   L _____

C _____   M _____

D _____   N _____

E _____   O _____

F _____   P _____

G _____   Q _____

H _____   R _____

I _____   S _____

J _____   T _____

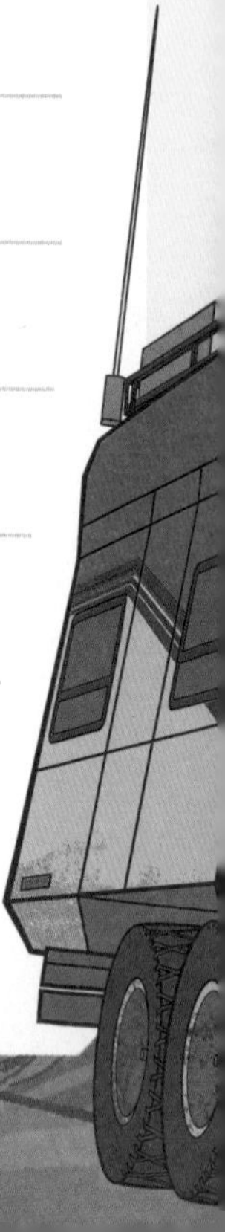

Find the letters of the alphabet outside the car, in order, starting with the letter **A**. You could find them on billboards, on store signs, on other cars, or emblazoned in the sky with fireballs. Well, that last one might be tricky.

Compete with others and see who can finish their own alphabet first, or play as a team.

U _____   X _____

V _____   Y _____

W _____   Z _____

ROUGH ROAD

HANG ALIEN

You probably know how to play hangman, but it's a bit more interesting with an alien. Instead of drawing a person, draw an alien. Think of a word between eight and twelve letters long. The alien will have:

A head   A third arm

A body   A leg

An arm   A second leg

A second arm   A tail

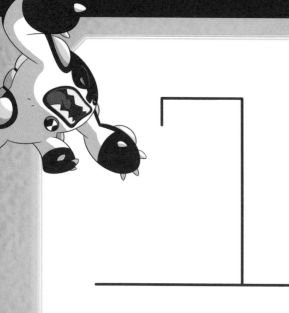

A J S
B K T
C L U
D M V
E N W
F O X
G P Y
H Q Z
I R

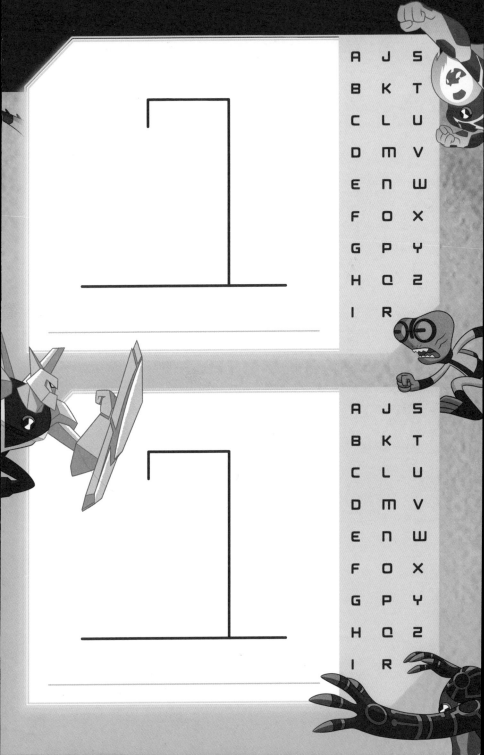

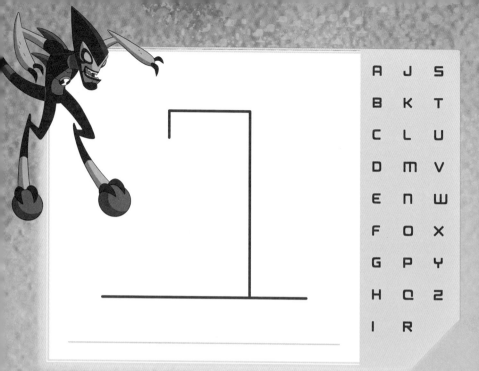

A J S
B K T
C L U
D M V
E N W
F O X
G P Y
H Q Z
I R

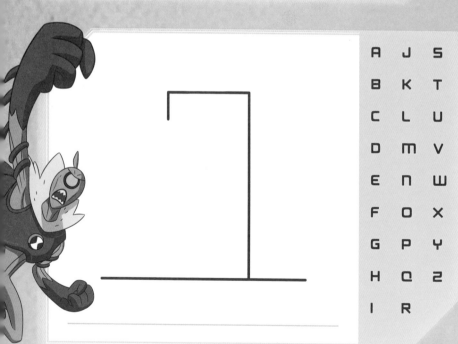

A J S
B K T
C L U
D M V
E N W
F O X
G P Y
H Q Z
I R

YOUR VERY OWN RUST BUCKET

The Rust Bucket is pretty cool, but I bet you could make one that looks even cooler. Feel free to give it a new coat of paint—it sure needs one!

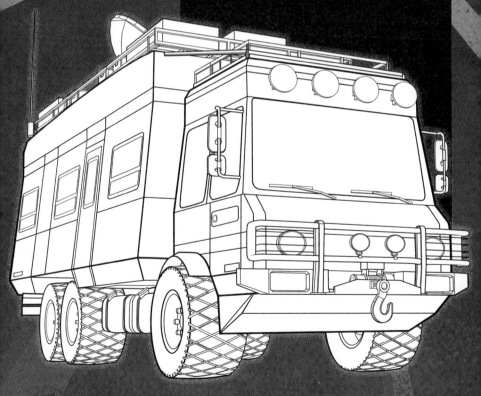

Your Ten

Ben has ten alien identities! What if you had some? What would one of them be, and what powers would you have?

Your alien name _____

The planet you are from _____

Your superpower _____

Say cheese! Draw your best alien self-portrait.

ROAD TRIP PLANNER

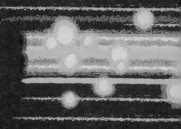

Imagine going on a long road trip without any video games. That would be awful! Going on a road trip means lots of planning. What would you pack?

Grab this checklist and make sure you got the right goods.

Camera _____

Music player _____

Sleeping bag _____

Pillow _____

Toothbrush _____

Underwear _____

Snacks (Which ones?) _____

_____

_____

Games (What games?) _____

_____

_____

Music (What songs?) _____

_____

_____

Books (Pick your favorites.) _____

_____

_____

Movies (Grab a few.) _____

_____

_____

Rust Bucket Mess

The Rust Bucket sure is messy.

Can you spot ten differences in these two pictures?

WHERE CAN YOU ESCAPE?

Hex is after you. Quick! Hide! Where can you go? Think of someplace he'll never find you.

Have other players try to guess where you're hiding, asking "yes" or "no" questions.

See how many questions it takes them to figure it out.

ALIEN SCRAMBLER

Someone has scrambled all of Ben's aliens.
Can you unscramble each one?

1. Nonboclant _____

2. Dadomanhide _____

3. Ofur Sarm _____

4. Tablehats _____

5. Vowelfor _____

6. Regy Temtar _____

7. Flintsky _____

8. Peardug _____

9. Livedwin _____

10. RX8L _____

Animo Farm

Dr. Animo has created a farm of hybrid creatures such as a half-wolf and half-sheep, and a pig with a second pig on his arm.

What sort of mutated creatures can you create?

CONNECT THE DOTS

The Rust Bucket's television isn't working. Luckily, Ben can upgrade the television to a whole new level of awesomeness, with the help of one of his alien alter egos.

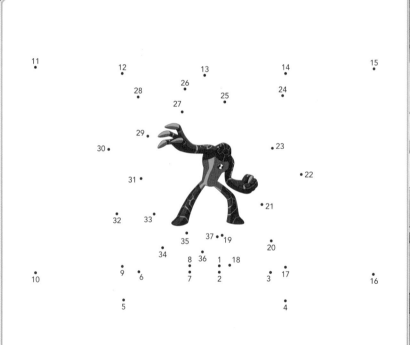

Guess Who #1?

I can create shockwaves merely by pounding my arms on the ground.

I can cross city blocks in a single jump.

I can defeat enemies with three hands behind my back.

Who am I? _____

LICENSE PLATE GAME

One thing Ben and Gwen like to do is to find as many state license plates as they can.

How many states can you find? Write your initial in each box when you spot a plate!

Dot Boxing

I HAVE WON THIS GAME 1,238 TIMES IN A ROW, BUT THEN AGAIN, I'M EXTREMELY BRILLIANT.

Each person takes a turn connecting two dots (horizontal or vertical, not diagonal). Keep connecting lines. When you create a line that forms a box, put the first letter of your first name in the box and go again. The game continues until every line is drawn. Whoever has completed the most boxes wins.

FIND THE VILLAINS

Bad guys seem to find me, but any superhero knows that sometimes you have to find the bad guys. Help me find some of my nemeses.

Hex

Zombozo

Maurice

Iron Kyle

Billy Billions

Clocktopus

Dr. Animo

Lord Decibel

Weatherheads

Steam Smythe

Simon

```
L V P S D R L F F V M D E C L
X D Z J D Y U I K A C H S M E
L C O A D A Y J U A T X L N B
V D M H N F E R U Y X J E T I
Y V B D D H I H M O W E P N C
N A O T I C W S R B X I S G E
K N Z U E Y M R A E U T C L D
N N O S Y A M B Q B H P H C D
I O J I E W L O V U R T Z M R
M A M T R O M I N A R D A A O
R H S I S O U W L K R U H E L
G C Y U S T N O N E Q F E W W
W A N S C A K K M M C Z O F M
S N O I L L I B Y L L I B M T
Z E M T H X P H X L H D F A V
B Z F V J G Y C N F E C Y H E
X S Q Q F B E M P D X L L I I
C L O C K T O P U S E Z T A V
B C V D Z V Z V W N H E S C N
Q D K Y H O I Z A I O E J V P
```

Tic-Tac-Toe, Alien-Style

Okay, everyone knows how to play this one, right? But let's play this one alien-style. Instead of **X**s and **0**s, draw pictures of Four Arms and Diamondhead!

Actually, that will be way too hard. Never mind. Just use **X**s and **0**s.

THE NEXT EVIL VILLAIN

Ben fights the strangest and baddest bad guys. Can you create your own bad guys who are just as evil?

Draw your own villain, describe his or her secret powers, and unveil his or her evil plans.

Name of villain _____

Evil weapon or power _____

Secret lair _____

Evil plan _____

_____

_____

_____

Looking good! Draw your evil-ness here.

Unfortunately/ Fortunately

This is a fun game to play with someone else. The first person makes an unfortunate statement, and then the next player makes the statement fortunate!

For example, the first player could say, "Unfortunately, that giant monster is going to eat us." The second player could then say, "Fortunately, I have an Omnitrix and will turn into Four Arms and defeat him."

What Unfortunately/Fortunately things can you come up with?

HELP BEN MAKE A MESS

The Rust Bucket is always a mess. This is what it looks like clean. Draw in lots of messes so it looks like home.

Super-Secret Alien Code

GWEN AND I CREATED OUR OWN CODE IN CASE WE EVER HAVE TO TALK WHEN I'M BATTLING VILLAINS. WE CAN USE THE CODE WHEN ... UM ... WELL, I'M NOT SURE, SINCE I'LL BE BATTLING VILLAINS AND WAY TOO BUSY TO USE THE CODE. BUT YOU CAN USE IT TO CRACK THIS SECRET MESSAGE I JUST MADE, ANYWAY.

HINT: Try "sliding" each letter one place forward in the alphabet.

'
_ _ _ _   _   _ _ _ _ _ _
F V D M   R   A Q D Z S G

_ _ _ _ _ _   _ _ _ _ _
R L D K K R   V N Q R D

_ _ _ _   _ _   _ _ _ _ _ _
S G Z M   L X   R S H M J X

_ _ _ _ _ .
R N B J R

THE ALPHABET GAME

Here's another road trip favorite. Pick a topic and then everyone takes turns naming something that begins with the letter **A**. Whoever lasts the longest wins that round. Then go to the letter **B**, and so on.

Here are topics. Each topic is its own game.

Animals

Places

Vehicles

TV characters

Food

Boy names

Girl names

Colors

Musicians or bands

Games

Books

Movies

Songs

Your Ten

Here's another chance to create your own alien. Ben has ten alien identities! What if you had some? What would one of them be, and what powers would you have?

Your alien name _____

The planet you are from _____

Your superpower _____

Show yourself, creature!

THE ANIMAL NAME GAME

This one is a little tricky, but it sure passes time on those long trips. One person names an animal. Then each person names another animal (no repeating!) that starts with the last letter of the previous animal. Keep going as long as you can!

Don't want to play animals? You can choose any of these categories:

Movies

Songs

Games

Food

Names

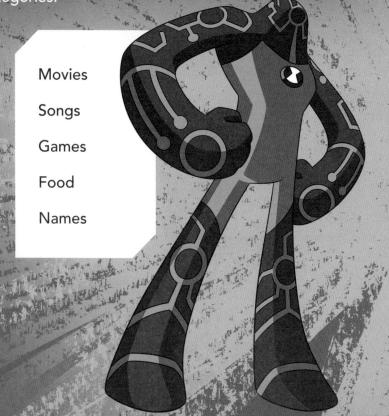

Grandpa Lessons

Below are two pictures of Grandpa Max lecturing Ben after Ben created another Rust Bucket mess. Can you spot ten differences between these pictures?

YUCK!

This is the Maggot Monster. That's right, it's a monster made from maggots. Could anything be more disgusting? Which alien do you think should fight it? Four Arms? Or how about Heatblast? Overflow?

Draw your favorite alien kicking this guy's butt!

Make sure you include lots of BAMs and POWs and stuff.

This should be epic!

SPEED RACING WITH XLR8

XLR8 is fast. Really fast. Like, blink-and-you'll-miss-him fast. So he needs to race through this maze fast. You have one minute to get from the beginning to the end. Do you think you can do it? Get your timer ready. On your mark, get set . . . go!

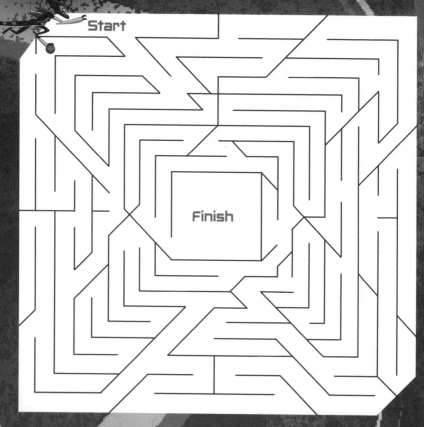

Your Uacation Planner

Okay, driving for hundreds of miles between places can be, well . . . boring. That would be okay, but some of the places we visit can be, well . . . boring, too!

You can probably pick a lot better places to go than Grandpa Max can!

Figure out where you want to go, what sights to see, and what you want to eat when you're there! Turn the page and start planning your trip, amigo!

Day One

Location: _____

Things to Do:

_____
_____
_____
_____

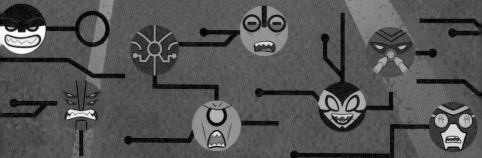

Things to See:

_____

_____

_____

_____

Things to Eat:

Breakfast: _____

Lunch: _____

Dinner: _____

Day Two

Location: _____

Things to Do:

_____

_____

_____

_____

Things to See:

_____

_____

_____

_____

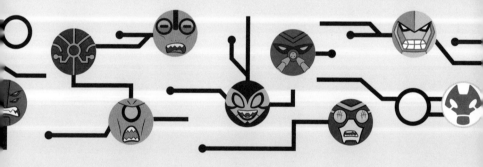

Things to Eat:

Breakfast: _____

Lunch: _____

Dinner: _____

Day Three

Location: _____

Things to Do:

_____

_____

_____

_____

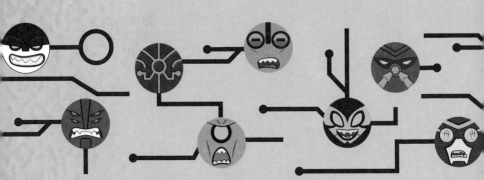

Things to See:

_____

_____

_____

_____

Things to Eat:

Breakfast: _____

Lunch: _____

Dinner: _____

Day Four

Location: _____

Things to Do:

_____
_____
_____
_____

Things to See:

_____

_____

_____

_____

Things to Eat:

Breakfast: _____

Lunch: _____

Dinner: _____

Day Five

Location: _____

Things to Do:

_____
_____
_____
_____

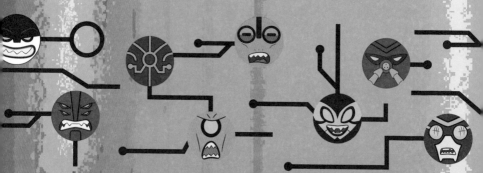

Things to See:

_____

_____

_____

_____

Things to Eat:

Breakfast: _____

Lunch: _____

Dinner: _____

THE GANG'S ALL HERE

Ben needs to find all his aliens to fight the giant Water Monster. Can you help him find them?

Cannonbolt

Diamondhead

Four Arms

Grey Matter

Heatblast

Overflow

Stinkfly

Upgrade

Wildvine

XLR8

```
C A N N O N B O L T D L E Q V
L S G R Q K P N O A O D C U W
N M V R O J K X E T A M D T P
J W X G E D N H Y R I W H U G
K O B U Y Y D T G E L F E K Y
Y C T U E N M P P W T V A K M
G L N X O G U A X L R 8 T F P
W H F M E C Q O T C N G B O R
B Y A K L F D W S T R F L M Q
V I J P N T P F Z F E P A Y M
D F S V N I O L Y D E R S L B
A N Y F D U T T T O N D T X Z
U S N M R O X S Y L I H Y D G
X D P A T B I P L C V D P I D
B X R R M D S F Z M D I N A T
M M P Q T D U S R L L C O E W
S F Y Z V N Y R C T I H R B F
D W O L F R E V O N W R G S I
D Q K P J V F H F U E A J O I
N C U S P T S Q W U G L I Y K
```

Guess Who #2?

I shoot slime.

You can smell me from a block away.

Criminals don't bug me at all.

Who am I? _____

Rust Bucket Road Fact

Did you know that the Rust Bucket is a type of Recreational Vehicle (RV)? Circle your favorite car. Can you draw a cooler one?

RECREATIONAL VEHICLE

CONVERTIBLE

SPORTS CAR

PICKUP TRUCK

JEEP

LUCKY GIRL

GWEN SOMETIMES DRESSES UP AS LUCKY GIRL, HER FAVORITE SUPERHERO. BUT I DON'T REALLY THINK GWEN HAS POWERS. SHE'S JUST LUCKY SOMETIMES. HOW LUCKY ARE YOU? LET'S SEE.

1. There are three glasses of milk. Two are poisoned. Which do you drink?

A. the one on the right

B. the one in the middle

C. the one on the left

2. Your friend bets you $10 on a flip of a coin. Which do you choose?

A. heads

B. tails

3. You find a haunted house with two stairways, one on the right and one on the left. One leads to your parents and one leads to a slime monster. Which direction do you choose?

A. right

B. left

4. A bomb is about to go off and blow up the city. You need to cut one of the wires to stop it. Do you cut the red or green wire?

A. red

B. green

5. You find three boxes. Two have a gas that will turn you into a snail. The other is safe. You open the box on the _____.

A. right

B. middle

C. left

6. A giant monster is about to eat the Rust Bucket. You can use fire or water to try to defeat him. Which do you choose?

    A. fire

    B. water

7. You're going to visit the Grand Canyon, but Grandpa Max is lost. The road forks up ahead. You tell Grandpa Max to go on the road to the _____.

    A. right

    B. left

Answer Key

1. The glass in the middle was not poisoned. Give yourself 1 point if you chose **B.**

2. The coin landed tails. Give yourself 1 point if you chose **B.**

3. Your parents were on the right. Give yourself 1 point if you chose **A.**

4. The red wire stops the bomb. Give yourself 1 point if you chose **A**.

5. The box on the right was safe. Give yourself 1 point if you chose **A**.

6. The monster was allergic to water. Give yourself 1 point if you chose **B**.

7. The road on the right led to the Grand Canyon. Give yourself 1 point if you chose **A**.

How lucky are you?

6-7 points: You could give Lucky Girl a run for her money. Maybe you should play the lottery.

4-5 points: You're not unlucky, but you're not exactly lucky, either. You're pretty normal. But that's okay. Still, you might not want to always trust your Ben-tuition.

0-3 points: Sorry to say this, but you're unlucky. Have any black cats passed your way recently? Remind me to stand away from you during a lightning storm.

Find the Titan Gauntlets

Hex wants the Titan Gauntlets. They can raise mountains and flatten them to the dust they came from! That doesn't sound good. Help Ben find them first.

YOUR BETTER RIDE

The Rust Bucket is awesome, but it's not the only vehicle that can take you places. How do you travel? Airplane? Submarine? Rocket ship?

Let's see what your perfect ride looks like!

Dot Boxing

You remember how to play this one, right? Each person takes a turn connecting two dots (horizontal or vertical, not diagonal). When you create a line that forms a box, put the first letter of your first name in the box and go again. The game continues until every line is drawn. Whoever has completed the most boxes wins.

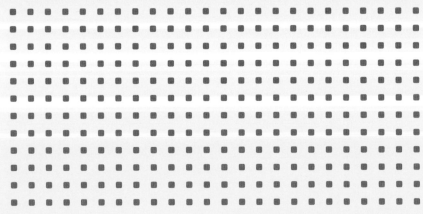

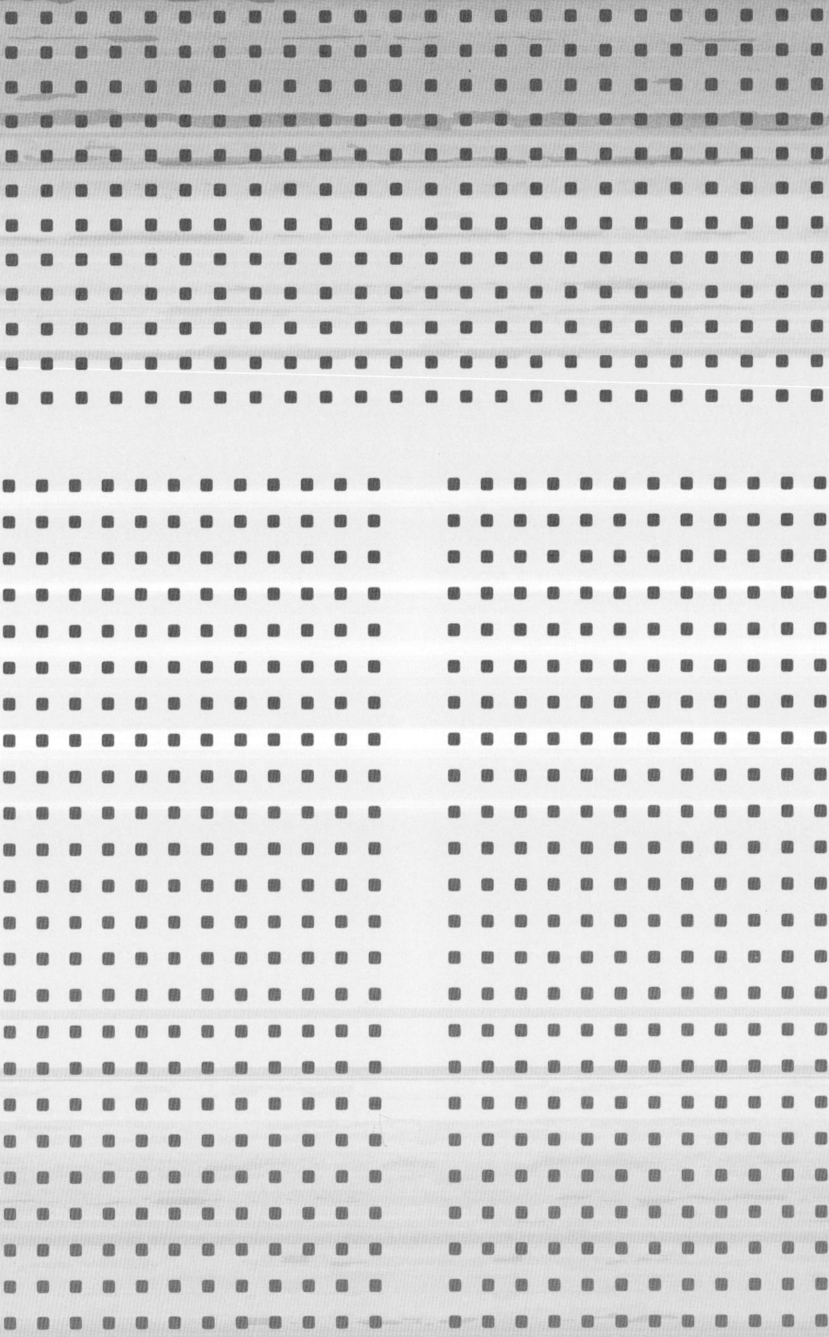

A SPELL OF TROUBLE

Grandpa Max and Gwen have been captured by Hex. He has created a horrible spell to capture them!

What spell?

I don't know, that's your job.

Grandpa Max and Gwen need help to escape—draw one of Ben's aliens saving the day!

How did they get into such a mess? Write your own *Ben 10* adventure with Hex capturing Gwen and Grandpa Max.

_____

_____

_____

_____

_____

_____

_____

_____

_____

_____

_____

_____

_____

_____

Guess Who #3?

I can throw crystals.

My arms can change shapes to form different weapons.

I can regrow my limbs.

Who am I? _____

DREAM LAND

Ben was awake for twenty-four hours watching season two of *Sumo Slammers*. Now he's finally fallen asleep.

Draw what he's dreaming about.

Rust Bucket Battleship

It's a battle of Rust Buckets between you and whoever is sitting next to you on your road trip.

Shade in four squares in a row. They have to be horizontal or vertical—they can't be diagonal. Now do that three more times. Those are your four Rust Buckets. Your opponent does this on the next page (no peeking).

Rust Buckets may not overlap.

Take turns firing on the enemy by calling out plot points (such as A-5). Your opponent will either say "hit" if you nailed one of his or her Rust Buckets, or "miss" if you didn't. Mark your shots as a "hit" (*H*) or as a "miss" (*M*) on your own sheet.

When your enemy fires on you, mark your hit Rust Buckets with an *X* when they are hit. When a Rust Bucket is destroyed (covered by four *X*s) say, "You destroyed my Rust Bucket!"

The first person to sink all of their enemy's Rust Buckets wins.

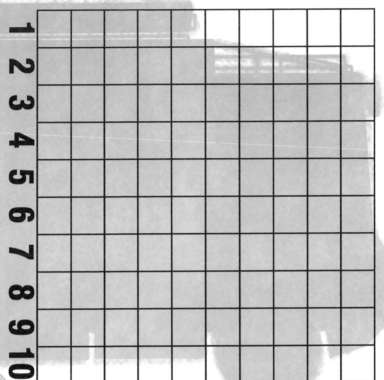

PLAYER A

A B C D E F G H I J
1 2 3 4 5 6 7 8 9 10

GAME 1

PLAYER B

	1	2	3	4	5	6	7	8	9	10
A										
B										
C										
D										
E										
F										
G										
H										
I										
J										

PLAYER A

A B C D E F G H I J

1 2 3 4 5 6 7 8 9 10

GAME 2

PLAYER B

A B C D E F G H I J

1 2 3 4 5 6 7 8 9 10

SPLASH ATTACK!

Cannonbolt is about to do a cannonball into the lake. Draw the splash when he hits. You might want to add stuff like fish flying out of the water, or maybe a sea serpent being awakened from a deep sleep.

SPECIAL SUPER-SECRET CODE

Someone has stolen the Rust Bucket. Luckily, we've found this secret code that reveals the villain. Can you help us discover who took our ride?

I SPY

Here's another chance to play I Spy. There's a lot going on outside! Spy something, give a hint, and see how long it takes the other players to figure out what you're spying.

Your Ten

Here's another chance to create your own alien. Ben has ten alien identities! What if you had some? What would one of them be, and what powers would you have?

Your alien name _____

The planet you are from _____

Your superpower _____

Lookin' awesome!

THE LICENSE PLATE ADDING GAME

Gwen and I play this a lot, although I usually do better when I'm Grey Matter.

Look at a license plate from any vehicle and add up all the numbers. For example, the license plate for the Rust Bucket is S81Z1M. Add the numbers only: 8 + 1 + 1 = 10.

Then add the numbers in your number, so 1 + 0 = 1.

One is your number. If that number appears in the license plate, you get a point! Then it's the next person's turn. Keep score and see who wins!

ONE STINKY PLANET

Stinkfly is a Lepidopterran from the world of Lepidopterra. I can't even pronounce it, but I'm sure it smells terrible.

Draw what you think it looks like.

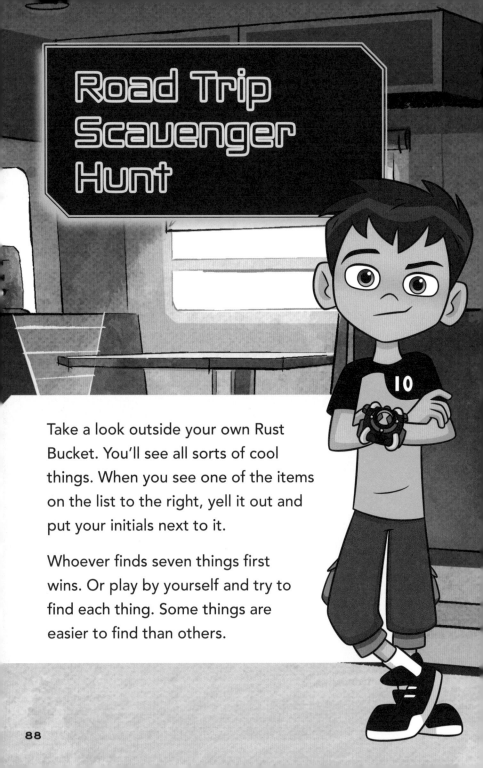

Road Trip Scavenger Hunt

Take a look outside your own Rust Bucket. You'll see all sorts of cool things. When you see one of the items on the list to the right, yell it out and put your initials next to it.

Whoever finds seven things first wins. Or play by yourself and try to find each thing. Some things are easier to find than others.

A sign with the letter **Q** in it _____

The number six _____

A twenty-foot alien frog _____

An airplane _____

A bridge _____

A construction sign _____

Hex _____

A cow _____

A horse _____

A stop sign _____

A barn _____

Keep going...!

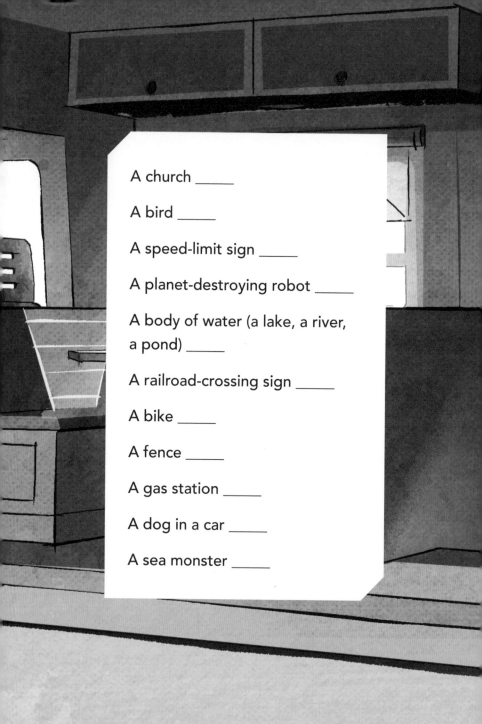

A church _____

A bird _____

A speed-limit sign _____

A planet-destroying robot _____

A body of water (a lake, a river, a pond) _____

A railroad-crossing sign _____

A bike _____

A fence _____

A gas station _____

A dog in a car _____

A sea monster _____

SIGHTSEEING SEARCH

Ben, Gwen, and Grandpa Max travel almost anywhere, even places that are hard to find. Can you find these popular places to visit?

Yellowstone

Central Park

White House

Disneyland

Times Square

Navy Pier

Hoover Dam

National Mall

Niagara Falls

Red Rock

```
M Y C C M G U N L N L Q A S T
A E I Q E N S B L V B Y L V I
D F Z A D N X H A D G L Q E M
R O A J B C T Z M F A T O J E
E W Q R W U N R L F D J C M S
V V U L X P O D A Z Y A U J S
O C D X W K S R N L W S X Y Q
O M R Q F Q A Q O H P I R T U
H D H I F G K P I Z R A A C A
Z P V Y A M Z T T H D O R F R
I V I I N V E K A O D I K K E
L D N U Y H M K N V E Y X C R
Y E L L O W S T O N E G E E Y
X I P U D N A L Y E N S I D Z
D X S N Q H J M U A Y P U C R
P E G Q F M G A K M Y X H B B
Q T W I A J D I P V W B T K X
R E D R O C K Y A M G M A Z Q
T G N R W K R N L F Q F K Y Y
E G N D E W V X B R F K Q B E
```

Guess Who #4?

I have a ball battling villains.

With my hard shell, I'm nearly invulnerable.

I can make quite a splash.

Who am I? _____

DID YOU HEAR THAT?

Did you hear that Four Arms defeated an army of lizards that were trying to eat Alabama?

Okay, not really. But you can play your own version of "did you hear that?"

- You start by asking, "Did you hear that _____ happened?" It can be a true statement or a false one.

- The next person can either say, "That didn't happen," "That did happen," or "Tell me more."

- If he or she correctly guesses that it did or didn't happen, that person gets two points.

- If that person guesses wrong, **you** get three points.

- If he or she asks, "Tell me more," then you give them a clue and the player can only get one point if they guess it right. But you still get three points if they guess it wrong.

INSTANT PHONE UPGRADE

Upgrade makes any technology more awesome. What if he upgraded your (or someone's) mobile phone? What extra powers could he give it?

Where in the World Is the Rust Bucket?

So, where are Ben, Gwen, and Grandpa Max now? What attraction are they visiting? Draw what they see!

CONNECT THE DOTS

It's not just getting somewhere, it's getting somewhere in style. After you connect the dots, draw in the details to make this picture even more awesome.

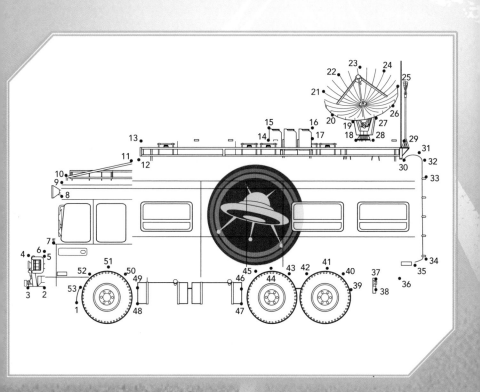

A Hex on You

Ben is fighting Hex. Can you spot the ten differences between these two pictures?

CAR SPIES

How good are you at spotting stuff? Take a look out the car window and see what other vehicles are on the road. Give yourself a point for every vehicle you find. Make it a game. Whoever finds the most stuff wins.

> *BEING A HERO MEANS SPOTTING EVIL BEFORE IT HAPPENS. IT'S EASY FOR ME BECAUSE I HAVE BEN-TUITION!*

❑ Tractor

❑ Tanker

❑ Pickup

❑ A green car

- ❑ Motorcycle
- ❑ Police car
- ❑ Semitruck
- ❑ Dump truck
- ❑ A yellow car
- ❑ Tow truck
- ❑ Bus
- ❑ Minivan
- ❑ Convertible
- ❑ A red car
- ❑ Cement truck
- ❑ Motor home
- ❑ Trailer
- ❑ Train
- ❑ Car carrier
- ❑ Taxicab

Match the Alien

Ben's Omnitrix is all messed up. Every time he picks an alien, he turns into a completely different alien.

Can you match the Omnitrix symbol with the real alien it is supposed to represent?

GROWING PAINS

Nanny Nightmare has created a baby powder that turns adults into babies, until Ben and Gwen reverse the powder's effects.

What if you were sprinkled with the powder that they reversed? Draw what you think you will look like when you're older.

Your Very Own License Plate

You see lots of license plates on the road, and a lot of them are pretty boring. We bet you could design one that is way more interesting.

First, come up with the name for your imaginary state or country. Then create your own license plate. Make one so cool that everyone will want it on their vehicle!

Dot Boxing

You already know this one. Each person takes a turn connecting two dots (horizontal or vertical, not diagonal). When you create a line that forms a box, put the first letter of your first name in the box and go again. The game continues until every line is drawn. Whoever has completed the most boxes wins.

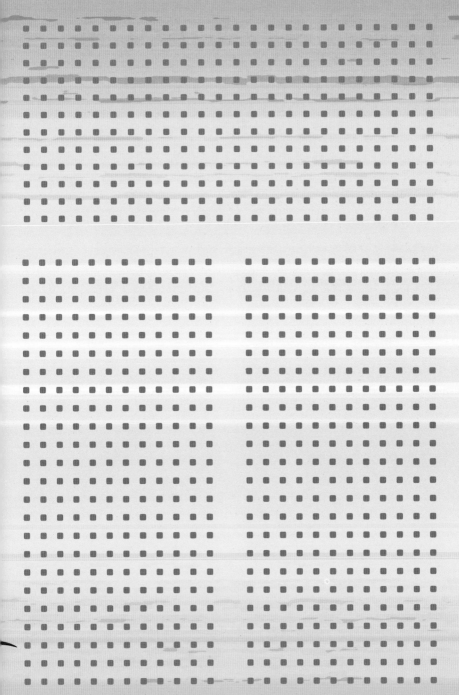

THE ALIEN IS . . . AWESOME!

To play, each player makes up a sentence around a letter of the alphabet, starting with **A**. You have to begin with the phrase "The alien is a _____." You have to use the letter **A** twice.

So the first player might say "The alien is an *awesome aardvark*." The second player replaces the two bold words with others starting with **A**, like, "The alien is an *adventurous ant*." If a player can't think of a new word, or if he or she repeats a word, he or she is out. The game continues with **B**, **C**, **D**, and so on.

CONNECT THE DOTS

This alien is buds with everyone. Plant yourself down, connect the dots, and see what sprouts up.

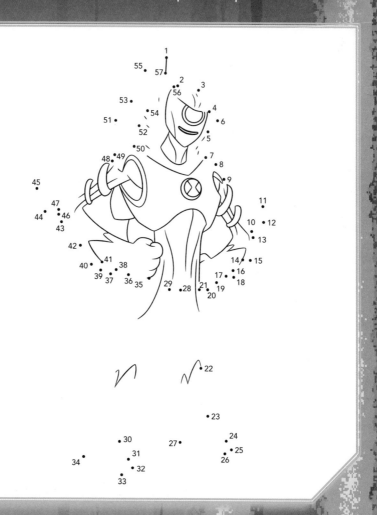

I'm Going On a Trip to an Alien Dimension

THIS IS A FUN MEMORIZATION GAME FOR TWO OR MORE PEOPLE, BUT AS GREY MATTER, NO ONE CAN BEAT ME. MY MEMORIZATION SKILLS ARE OUT OF THIS WORLD...LITERALLY.

The first person repeats the line "I'm going on a trip to an alien dimension, and I'm bringing . . ." He or she finishes the line with nearly anything—but it needs to be two words long, with each word beginning with the letter **A**. So you could say, "I'm going on a trip to an alien dimension, and I'm bringing awesome aardvarks!"

The next person repeats the opening line, what the last person just said, and what they will bring. But now each word begins with the letter **B**.

You keep going down the alphabet. If someone forgets anything, they're out.

ANSWER KEY

page 6
Can You Help Ben Find Zombozo?

page 18 • Rust Bucket Mess

pages 20–21 • Alien Scrambler:
Cannonbolt, Diamondhead, Four Arms, Heatblast, Overflow, Grey Matter, Stinkfly, Upgrade, Wildvine, XLR8

page 24 • Connect the Dots

page 25 • Guess Who #1?
Four Arms

page 29 • Find the Villains

```
L V P S D R L F F V M D E C L
X D Z J D Y U I K A C H S M E
L C O A D A Y J U A T X L N B
V D M H N F E R U Y X J E T I
Y V B D D H I M M O W E P N C
N A O T I C W S R B X I S G E
K N Z U E M R A E U T C L D
N N O S Y A M B Q B H P H C D
I O J I E W L O V U R T Z M R
M A M T R O M I N A R D A A O
R H S A S O U W L K R U H E L
G C Y U S T N O N E Q F E W W
W A N S C A K K M M C Z O F M
S N O I L L I B Y L L I B M T
Z E M T H X P H X L H D F A V
B Z F V J G Y C N F E C Y H E
X S Q Q F B E M P D X L L I I
C L O C K T O P U S E Z T A V
B C V D Z V Z V W N H E S C N
Q D K Y H O I Z A I O E J V P
```

pages 36–37 • Super-Secret Alien Code:
GWEN'S BREATH SMELLS WORSE THAN MY STINKY SOCKS.

page 43 • Grandpa Lessons

page 46 Speed Racing With XLR8

page 58 • The Gang's All Here

```
C A N N O N B O L T D E Q V
L S G R Q K P N O A O D C U W
N M V R Q J K X E T A M D T P
J W X G E D N H Y R I W H U G
K O B U Y Y D T G E L F E K Y
Y C T U E N M P P W T V A K M
G L N X O G U A X L R B T F P
W K F M E C Q O T C N G B O R
B Y A K L F D W S T R F L M Q
V I J F N T P F Z F E R A Y M
D F S V N I O L Y D E R S L B
A N Y F D U T T O N D T X Z
U S N M R O X S Y L I H Y D G
X D P A T B I P L C V D P I D
B X R R M D S F Z M D I N A T
M M P Q T D U S R L L C O E W
S F Y Z V N Y R C T I H R B F
D W O L F R E V O N W R G S I
D Q K P J V F H F U E A J O I
N C U S P T S Q W U G L I Y K
```

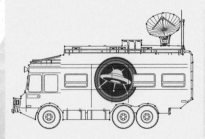